SCHMITT

Written by Gavin Rhodes
Illustrated by Tatiana Furlan

Dear mimi,

Hope you enjoy the book!
Happy reading :)
All the best
   Gavin Rhodes

Published by New Generation Publishing in 2019

Copyright © Gavin Rhodes 2019

First Edition

The author asserts the moral right under the Copyright, Designs and Patents Act 1988 to be identified as the author of this work.

All Rights reserved. No part of this publication may be reproduced, stored in a retrieval system or transmitted, in any form or by any means without the prior consent of the author, nor be otherwise circulated in any form of binding or cover other than that which it is published and without a similar condition being imposed on the subsequent purchaser.

ISBN: 978-1-78955-536-3

www.newgeneration-publishing.com

New Generation Publishing

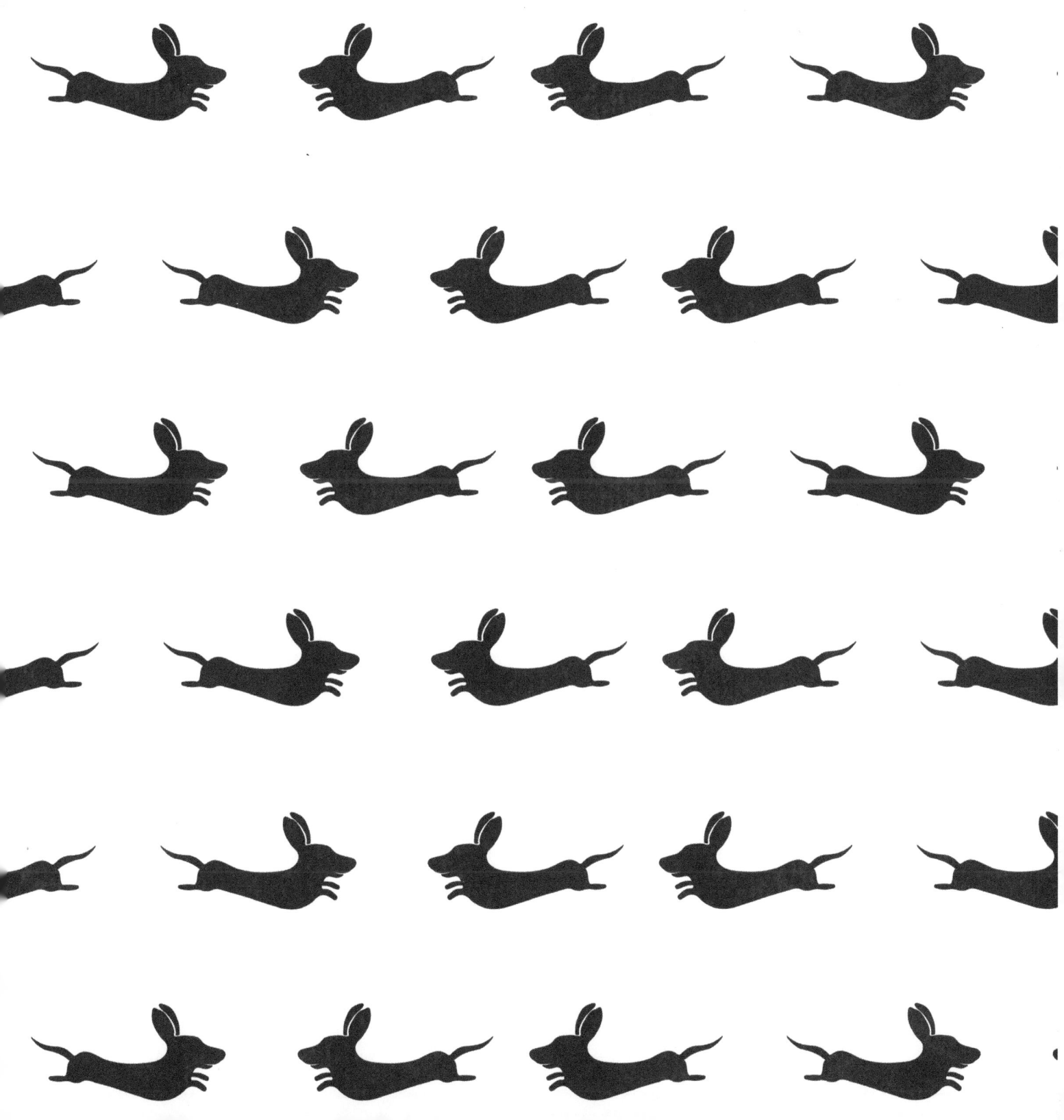

Schmitt goes to the park

It was a glorious morning and the sun was BEAMING.
Schmitt was in a deep sleep, lazily DREAMING.

'Walkies!' Bethany said with GLEE.
Schmitt opened one eye very SLOWLY.

'It's lovely outside, let's GO!'
A growl came from the little pup
followed by a grumpy… 'NO.'

Suddenly Schmitt's nose started twitching,
thanks to the smell of a freshly baked CAKE.

He quickly jumped up, with a spring in his step,
Schmitt was finally AWAKE!

'That's not for you, paws off SCHMITT!'
Giving Bethany his puppy-dog eyes...
'Oh just a BIT?!'

'You need some exercise,'
Bethany said dangling the house KEYS.
'Most dogs like going out for WALKIES!'

'It will be fun, and maybe after
there will be a nice juicy BONE.'
'Grrrr okay,' said Schmitt in his husky TONE.

Schmitt finally made his way outside
and with a frown he waddled AROUND,
He really was a soppy HOUND.

'Fetch!' shouted Bethany whilst
launching a tennis BALL,
But Schmitt had
no interest in it at ALL.

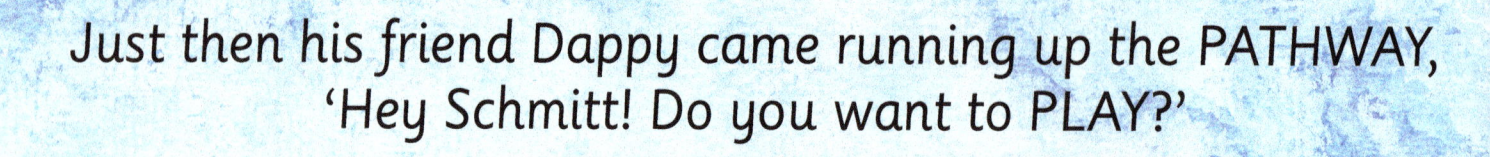

Just then his friend Dappy came running up the PATHWAY,
'Hey Schmitt! Do you want to PLAY?'

'We can run and dodge and RACE!
Come on Schmitt, just look at all this SPACE!'

Schmitt suddenly perked up
and responded with a BARK.
And the two pups began to chase each other
all over the PARK.

Schmitt returned to Bethany panting,
then produced a big SMILE.
'I feel great,' he said, 'I haven't done that in a WHILE.'

It seemed that Schmitt
had forgotten all about the BONE,
And now he didn't want to go HOME.

So, although Schmitt
didn't start the day being very WISE,
He soon realised that it's good to EXERCISE.

From that day on Schmitt became a lot more active and HAPPY,
Largely down to his good pal DAPPY.

Exercising is healthy and FUN.
So, don't be a slouch, get some fresh air and go for a RUN.

Schmitt gets it wrong

It was a stormy NIGHT,
Schmitt woke with a FRIGHT.

He was having that
bad dream AGAIN,
The one with
the huge Great DANE.

He had the same dream a LOT,
Waking each time sweaty and HOT.

Under his pillow he had to HIDE,
The little dog was PETRIFIED.

The next morning Schmitt sat with Bethany on her CHAIR,
And told her all about his horrible NIGHTMARE.

Bethany chuckled,
'You have never even seen a dog of that KIND,
Only from dreams inside your MIND.'

'I have seen one!' insisted Schmitt,
'On TV of COURSE!
A giant scary looking dog
the size of a HORSE.'

Bethany replied,
'Yes, Great Danes are
a much bigger BREED,
But don't be afraid,
there's really no NEED.'

'Well you didn't see my dream,
it wasn't FUN,
I hope I never meet ONE!'

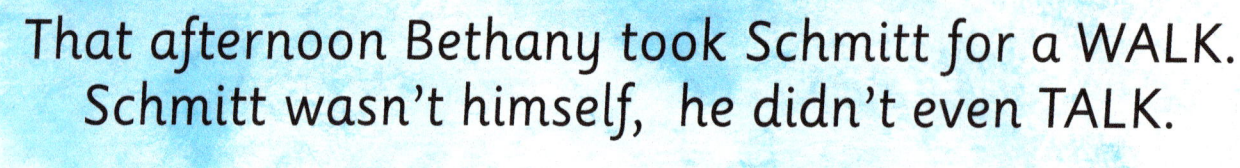

That afternoon Bethany took Schmitt for a WALK.
Schmitt wasn't himself, he didn't even TALK.

As they walked along the street, Bethany said,
'Let's take the short cut TODAY.'
Schmitt looked up... '
You mean the ALLEYWAY?'

'It's fine you silly DOGGY.'
'Really?' said Schmitt, 'It's a bit FOGGY.'

'It's perfectly safe,
everyone takes this PATH.'
'Okay,' said Schmitt
with a nervous LAUGH.

Halfway through
and Schmitt noticed
the alley was not very WIDE.
Just then, a lady entered
from the other SIDE.

She stepped forward
holding a lead and from behind
her came a loud BARK.
Then a big animal appeared
from out of the DARK.

Schmitt started to SWEAT,
This did not look like
an ordinary PET!

It was a Great Dane! Schmitt's dream was REAL.
'Oh Schmitt!' said Bethany, 'It's no big DEAL.'

Schmitt was trembling like never BEFORE,
His paws seemed to be stuck to the FLOOR.

The huge dog approached with a smile and a pink bow on its HEAD!
Then with a soft calming voice, 'Excuse me,' she SAID.

Schmitt stared at her ginormous front paws, they were very well groomed and a lovely shade of GREY.
'I'm awfully sorry,' she said, 'I would like to pass if I MAY?'

Schmitt was surprised to say the LEAST.
She was delightful, far from a scary BEAST.

He swiftly let her THROUGH.
'That's ever so kind, thank YOU.'

'Come along Daisy!'
the elegant lady CRIED.
Daisy strolled on with her
long and graceful STRIDE.

'I told you Schmitt,' stated Bethany,
'Great Danes are really nice.
Now do you SEE?!'
Schmitt smiled, 'Yes, I have to AGREE!'

Great Danes were fierce and terrifying in Schmitt's EYES,
He believed this because of their SIZE.

First impressions can often MISLEAD,
You shouldn't always believe what you watch or READ.

It's normal to look at the appearance of ANOTHER,
But please, oh please, don't judge a book by its COVER.

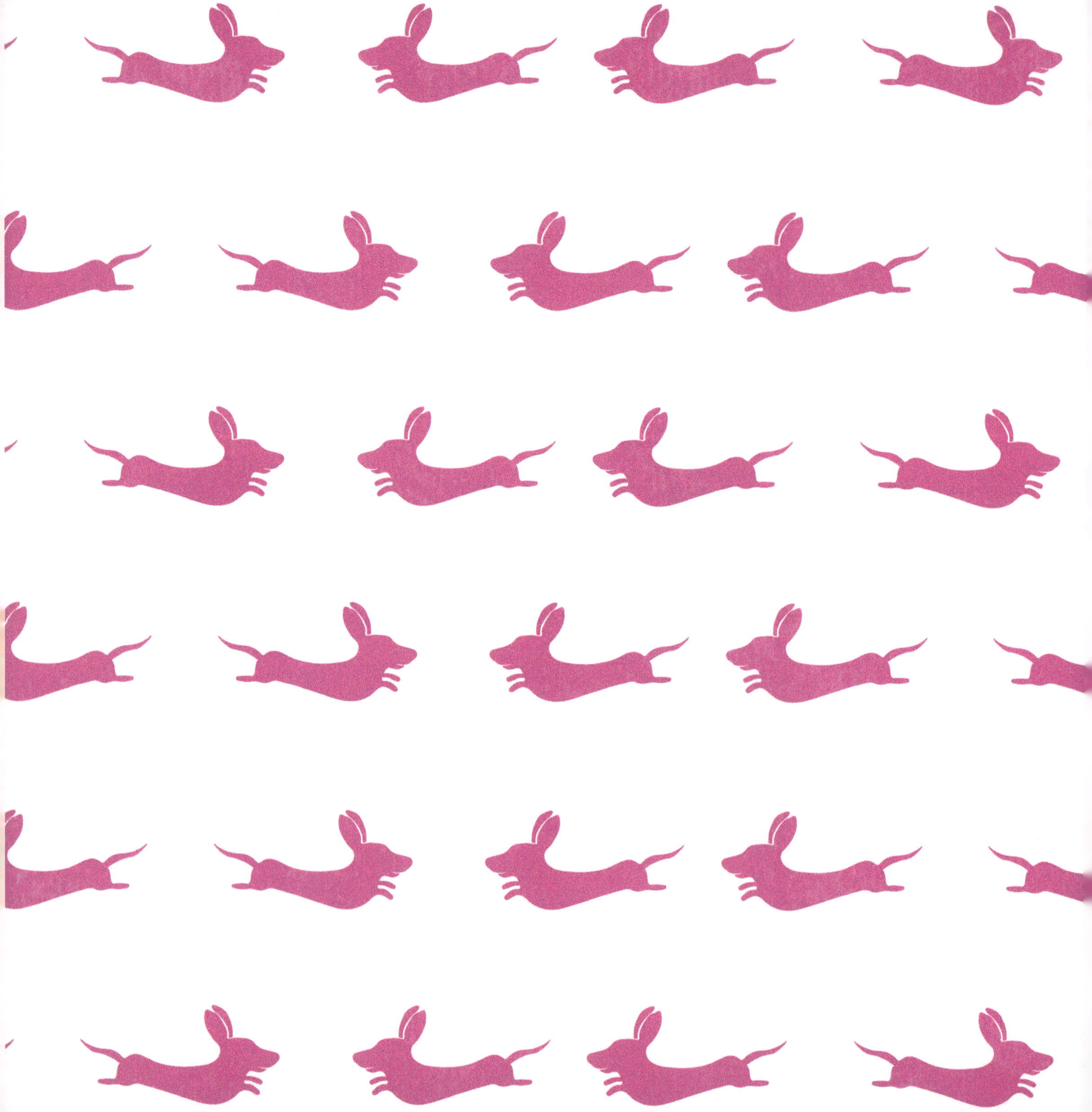

Schmitt takes on a challenge

'Okay!' said Bethany,
'I have signed us up for a charity mountain TREK.'
Schmitt gulped, 'Err I think I'll take a rain CHECK!'

'Don't be silly,' Bethany replied, 'it will be GREAT.
It's in two weeks, and I can't WAIT.'

Schmitt's ears flopped over his big brown EYES.
'I've only got little legs, are you sure this is WISE?!'

'Well, we must practice and train
so we are ready for the big DAY.'
Schmitt did not seem particularly excited
it's fair to SAY.

'You'll be fine, and anyway
it's for a good CAUSE.'
Schmitt gave a weary smile as he rested on his PAWS.

The next morning, Bethany and Schmitt
were ready to TRAIN.
Schmitt's face was a picture as he peered
outside at the RAIN.

They started by walking up steps and a mighty steep HILL,
Then on to the gym where they tried the TREADMILL.

After the first day Schmitt was
grumpy and worn OUT.
The trek was going to be tough
for him there was no DOUBT.

Each day Schmitt
was put to the TEST.
He struggled but certainly
tried his BEST.

The day of the trek was finally HERE,
Schmitt and Bethany were all dressed in their GEAR.

They were ready for the challenge
that lay AHEAD.
Schmitt wasn't keen at first,
but now he was positive INSTEAD.

As they approached the start of the trek, there were many people looking fit and LEAN. The mountain was in the distance— the highest Schmitt had ever SEEN.

Off they went feeling GOOD. Schmitt wanted to reach the top and was confident he COULD.

Halfway up the mountain the pair
were in their STRIDE.
'Good boy Schmitt,'
Bethany said with PRIDE.

As they got higher,
Schmitt was starting to feel a bit QUEEZY,
He really wasn't finding this EASY.

'Can we go BACK?
I'm ready for some TV and a SNACK.'

'I'm sorry to be a BORE,
But I just can't walk ANYMORE.'

'But Schmitt!' Bethany replied, 'you have come so FAR.
You can do it, you're a little STAR.'

'I'm not sure about THAT,
My battery is FLAT!'

'Don't worry,'
Bethany replied with sympathy,
'I can carry you the rest of the WAY.'
Schmitt smiled and replied, 'OKAY!'

And with the weary pup on Bethany's BACK,
Schmitt watched the other trekkers moving along the TRACK.

He paused for a moment and then shouted…'STOP THERE!
I want to walk,' he did DECLARE.

'We've trained too hard for me to QUIT,
I will find the energy from somewhere, I'll make sure of IT.'

'I can't give up just like THAT.'
Bethany lowered him down and gave him a gentle PAT.

Schmitt was now focused on reaching the TOP,
And despite his struggles he was determined not to STOP.

He tried with all his MIGHT,
And now the peak was in SIGHT.

One final push and they finally reached the SUMMIT,
Schmitt and Bethany had DONE IT!

It was certainly a hard SLOG,
But they raised lots of money
for 'Help a Stray DOG'.

Schmitt was tired but
glad he didn't QUIT.
He showed real determination
and a lot of GRIT.

Some goals will be
hard to ACHIEVE,
Don't be too quick to give up,
always BELIEVE.

Striving for the top and giving it your ALL,
One day you'll reap rewards both big and SMALL.

Without perseverance, you won't get very FAR,
Give yourself a chance to be a SUPERSTAR.

Gavin Rhodes, author of the popular Children's Book Series 'Superstar Kids' writes stories inspired by his children and experiences as a father. Gavin's rhyming stories focus on providing his young audience with a fun, relatable and educational way of teaching valuable life lessons. His unique style has attracted all types of fans worldwide including royalty!

Tatiana Furlan is a versatile artist passionate about traditional children's illustration and animation. The majority of her work is made in watercolors on paper. She graduated in Venice in History of Art and previously she received a Diploma in Graphic Design. Tatiana's art is inspired by her life experiences, wellbeing, and natural elements bringing the most fun and colorful side of those.

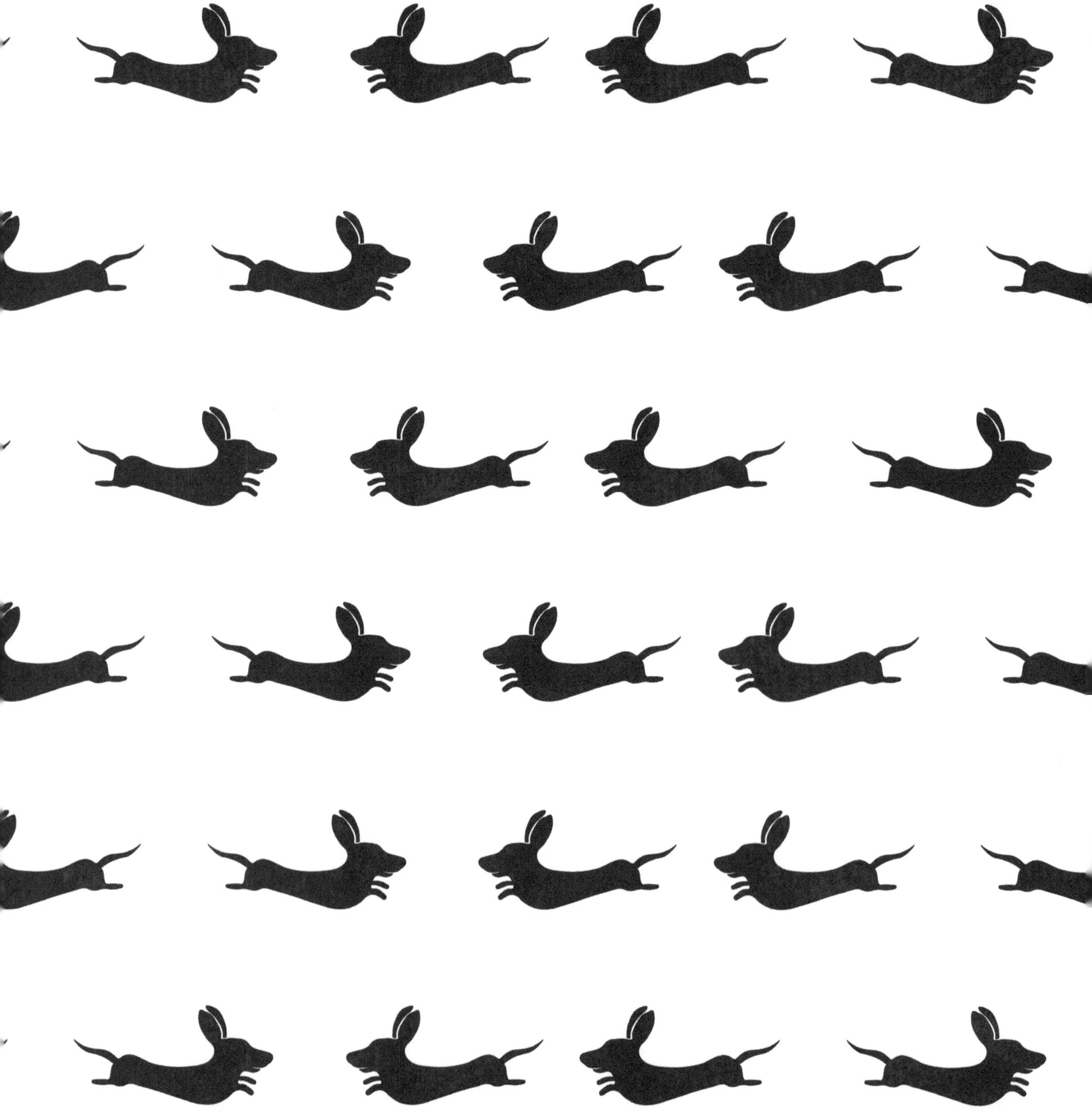

Lightning Source UK Ltd.
Milton Keynes UK
UKHW020836240919
350291UK00005B/84/P